Cuthbert
and the
Merpeople

by
Kathy Mezei

Drawings by Anne Stratford

CACANADADADA

Kathy Mezei is a professor in the English Department at Simon Fraser University in Burnaby, British Columbia, and specializes in Canadian Literature. She wrote *Cuthbert* one summer while camping on Hornby Island. Every day she would take her daughter, Robin, out in a canoe, tell her an episode, and then hurry back to shore where she would quickly type it up on her portable typewriter.

Anne Stratford is an artist and travelling ESL teacher who loves communicating through different languages, pictures and acting. That *Cuthbert and the Merpeople* should be her first illustrated book seems especially appropriate; as a child, she longed to be a mermaid when she grew up. Anne Stratford is presently learning from and teaching students in grade six in the Ungava Bay area.

CACANADADADA PRESS LTD.
3350 West 21st Avenue
Vancouver, B.C. Canada
V6S 1G7

Typesetting: The Typeworks, Vancouver, B.C.
Printing: Hignell Printing, Winnipeg, Manitoba
Cover Design: Anne Stratford & Cecilia Jang
Cover Art: Anne Stratford
Set in Novarese, 14 pt. on 20

The publisher wishes to thank the Canada Council for its generous financial assistance.

Canadian Cataloguing in Publication Data

Mezei, Kathy, 1947-
    Cuthbert and the merpeople

    ISBN 0-921870-18-3

    I. Stratford, Anne.   II. Title.
PS8576.E94C8 1992   jc813'.54   C92-091468-3
PZ7.M494Cu 1992

for Robin, of course

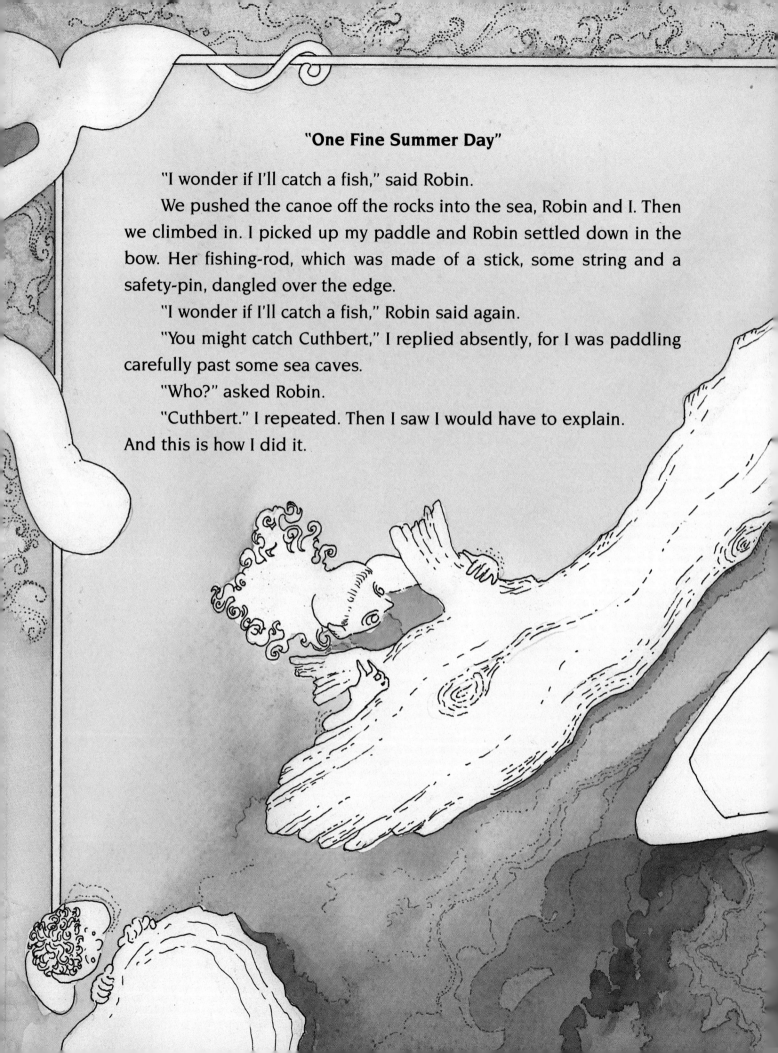

"One Fine Summer Day"

"I wonder if I'll catch a fish," said Robin.

We pushed the canoe off the rocks into the sea, Robin and I. Then we climbed in. I picked up my paddle and Robin settled down in the bow. Her fishing-rod, which was made of a stick, some string and a safety-pin, dangled over the edge.

"I wonder if I'll catch a fish," Robin said again.

"You might catch Cuthbert," I replied absently, for I was paddling carefully past some sea caves.

"Who?" asked Robin.

"Cuthbert." I repeated. Then I saw I would have to explain. And this is how I did it.

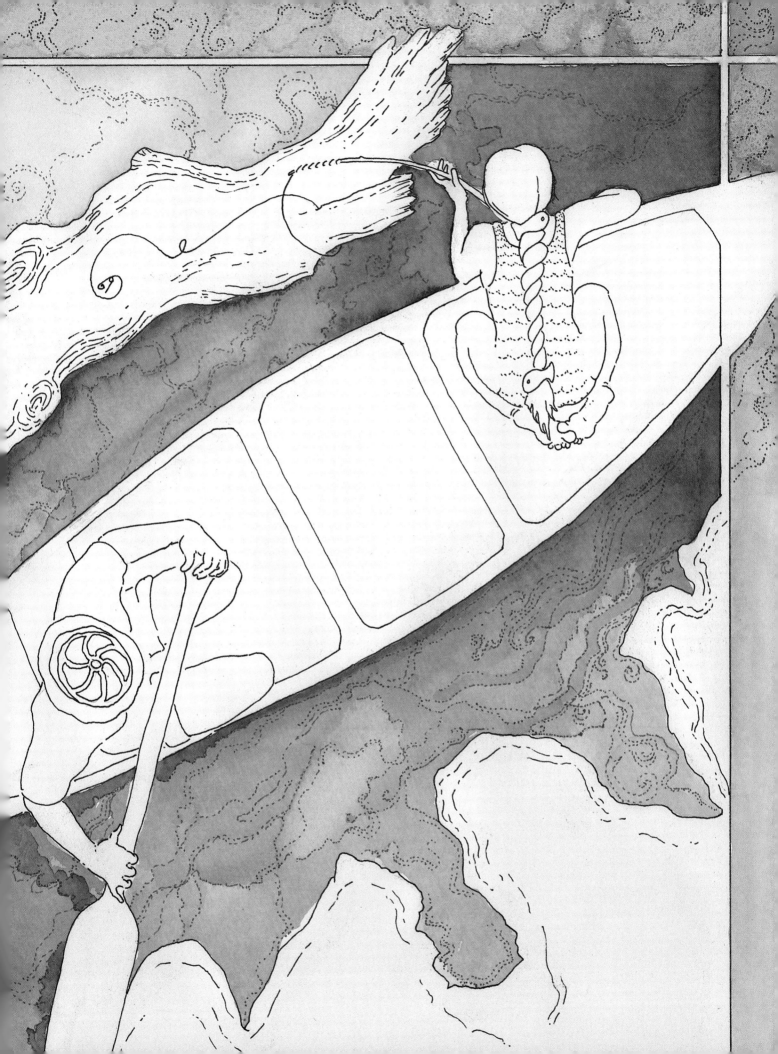

The Merpeople of Hornby Island

A long time ago, mermaids and mermen frolicked on the rocks and seas by Hornby Island. This was long before people lived there. Then only deer wandered about the island, while seals and fish and whales swam undisturbed in the ocean. Here, in a sheltered cove, lived the MerQueen and MerKing of the island, with their children, Miranda and Toby. Their palace lay in a maze of tunnels and caves under the sea. Its entrance was hidden among rocks at the sea's edge. At the very end of the tunnels, far beyond the sea palace, was an enormous cave, the size of a small city.

The merfamily lived happily in their sea palace, and although it was dark so far beneath the sea . . .

("Maybe," Robin interrupted, "they had lamp fish to light it all up."

"You're right," I said.)

. . . hundreds of shocking pink and fluorescent orange lamp fish swam back and forth, lighting up the palace so they could cook and read and comb their long tresses before going to sleep at night.

Then Cuthbert the sea monster came. And everything was different, terribly different.

How Cuthbert Came to Hornby Island

On the other side of the world in Scotland lived Cuthbert.

Cuthbert was Nessie's eldest son . . . Nessie, the famous and mysterious sea monster of Loch Ness. Cuthbert was handsome, but vain and wilful. He had shiny black hair, seven lovely symmetrical loops, big soft eyes, a nice pink mouth and two rows of pearly white teeth. He was a very large sea monster, almost as long as two city blocks.

One day, Cuthbert said to Nessie, "I want tae visit ma cousins in Loch Linnhe." Loch Linnhe was the next loch over from Loch Ness, connected by a secret underwater tunnel.

Nessie cautiously rose to the surface, raised one eye just a tiny bit

above the loch waters, then sank back down to the muddy, chilly bottom.

"No, Cuthbert," she said firmly. "It's too calm; ye ken I dinna like any of the family to appear when it's calm because the folks see us and get all flummoxed and rush about in a panic. Wait for a stoury day, then no one will notice."

Cuthbert pouted, and when Cuthbert pouted ripples rose from his pout to the surface of the loch causing six-foot waves which scattered a school of fish at their early morning lessons. Shaking her head crossly and muttering, "I telt you so," Nessie curled down for her afternoon nap. But when she was snoring loudly, Cuthbert slithered along the loch's bottom to the tunnel to Loch Linnhe. All afternoon he played with his cousins, first tag, then hide and seek among the reeds at the bottom of the loch and, best of all, somersaults which made them delightfully queasy.

When he returned, late for supper, Nessie was furious. "This'll no do at all. While I reign as the Queen of Loch Ness, indeed of all the lochs of Scotland, you will obey me, or else!" She even went so far as to spank Cuthbert, which was quite difficult as she had no hands, and it was hard to tell which of his loops was his behind.

"Dinna you tell me what to dae! I'm big now!" Cuthbert raged.

"As long as you bide in my loch, you will do as I tell you," answered his mother.

("Oh, oh," said Robin. "Then he'll have to leave.")

"Then I'm gonna leave!" shouted Cuthbert.

With that he opened the secret gate that led from Loch Ness to the North Sea, swam through, and slammed it shut behind him.

Suddenly he was in the cold, dark North Sea. He had never seen such space or so many fish and whales. He wiggled his loops in delight though it was cold, colder even than Loch Ness. He made his way north

till he could not tell the difference between day and night, and only the cold twinkling of the stars lit his way. He swam towards the North Pole through the Northwest Passage that joined the cold north Atlantic to the cold north Pacific. When he poked his astonished head through the ice, he saw polar bears squatting on icebergs fishing with their paws, and arctic wolves howling at the moon. On and on Cuthbert swam, past the gleaming North Pole, past a pod of great white whales singing to each other. Then he turned south through the Bering Sea and soon there were fewer and fewer icebergs.

It was time to find a home, for he was tired and a little lonely. He missed his mother, and he was rather sorry now that he had been so rude, leaving without a proper good-bye.

After a while he saw an island, and its green forests and rocks and clouds of mist reminded him of Scotland. His heart thumped and his loops quivered with joy. Maybe this could be a home for him? He swam round and round the island. He stuck his soft snout into every crevice, looking for a passageway into the bowels of the island, for he needed tunnels and caves deep beneath the sea where he could hide. Like most sea monsters he was quite shy.

Alas for the merfamily, he found their cave entrance. It was a bit of a tight squeeze, but once he got in he swam excitedly through the tunnels until he found the big cave at the end, the cave like a small city.

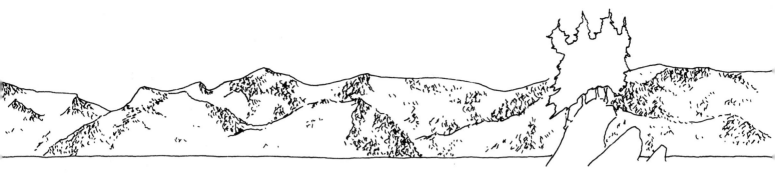

Suddenly the merfamily's life changed. Whenever Cuthbert slithered past, they hid in the palace, shaking with fright. The lamp fish were too nervous to glow, and the palace grew dark and gloomy. Miranda and Toby were afraid to play in the undersea tunnels. When Cuthbert splashed about in the sea, they didn't dare to sunbathe on the rocks. Not one of their cousins would visit them. The aunts and uncles politely declined the MerKing's invitations for dinner. For safety the merfamily went everywhere with an escort of sharks.

However, after Cuthbert ate his fill of fish, he got sleepy. Yawning, he crawled into his cave and slept for at least three months. Because he snored so loudly, the merfamily always knew when he was sleeping, and took up their former carefree life again. Just in case, though, they posted ten electric eels at the mouth of Cuthbert's cave. The eels watched while Cuthbert slept, and when he began to stir, they slid back to the sea palace to warn the merfamily. When Cuthbert woke, snorting and shaking and stretching, loud rumbles echoed through the caves like a minor earthquake. The merfamily trembled and quaked too. As they hid in the dungeons of their palace, Cuthbert sleepily glided past, out to the open sea for a little exercise and breakfast.

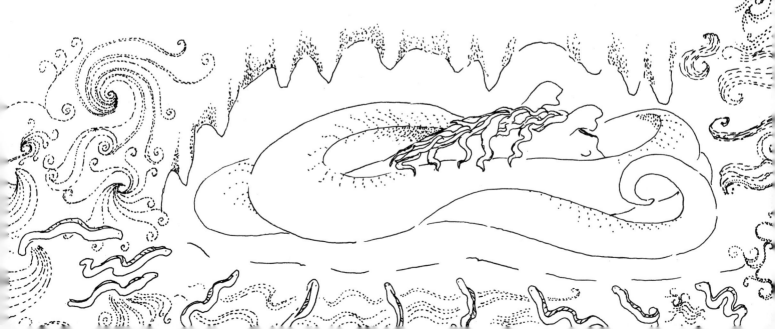

Miranda Makes a Decision

"This can't go on," said Miranda to Toby as they were lying on the rocks under the hot noon sun. Cuthbert was having one of his three-month naps.

"What can't?" asked Toby, sleepily, opening one eye.

Miranda sat up, gracefully curling her tail under her. She tossed back her long green hair. She had big green eyes and a lovely green tint to her skin. "Us being terrorized by that sea monster."

"But what can we do?" asked Toby, turning over to tan his back a darker green.

"I think we should do battle."

"Battle?" Toby was doubtful.

"Yes, we could get the sharks—that's twenty sharks—the electric eels—that's ten—mother and father and us—that's four and," she added triumphantly, "our mercousins on the other side of the island—that's ten!"

Toby counted his fingers—he had no toes—and then he counted Miranda's and then his again. "Twenty-five altogether!"

Miranda was skeptical. "That doesn't sound right."

He tried again. "How about forty-one?"

"That sounds better."

"But what would we do?" asked Toby.

Miranda then dived into the sea with a tremendous splash. "Look what we can do!" She swam in a circle round and round, very fast, then did a double flip in the air, and a triple somersault under the sea. Toby dived in beside her and did a triple flip in the air, and a double somersault under the waves.

Far away on the horizon, two whales swimming by paused to watch. "Aren't they graceful!" said one to the other.

Miranda finally stopped flipping and leaped up onto a rock. Picking up a dry starfish, she began to comb her tresses. Toby climbed up beside her and shook the seaweed out of his hair.

"But what about the battle?"

("Why not have the sharks with their teeth bite the sea monster and the electric eels electric him?" interjected Robin, as we were canoeing by the entrance to the merfamily's cave.

"I don't think that would really get rid of Cuthbert for good," I said.

"Then they could do it every day," suggested Robin.)

But Miranda had another idea. "We'll call a council meeting," she said. "Here at the sea palace, and mother and father will preside. All the cousins and aunts and uncles will come to discuss strategy."

Toby looked up at his sister. "Good idea!"

(But Robin interrupted again as were drifting through the kelp. "I have a better idea. Why don't the merchildren talk to Cuthbert and see if they can be friends instead?"

"That *is* a good idea," I said, picking up my paddle, "but I don't think Miranda and Toby have thought of that . . . yet.")

The Merchildren Fetch Their Cousins

With three flips of her strong tail, Miranda dived off the rocks into the sea. Toby followed. First they swam to Spray Point where their cousins lived. Miranda surfaced, shaking the water from her hair and eyes.

"We're calling a council meeting for tonight at the Great Hall in the sea palace."

"Fine," said the cousins who were having tea on the rocks. "We'll be there and we'll bring seaweed stew with oyster bits."

Miranda and Toby swam on to Norris Rocks, where their aunt and uncle lived. "We're calling a council meeting," Miranda called up, "at the Great Hall in the sea palace. Tonight."

"Good, we'll be there," waved their aunt and uncle. "We'll bring sea lettuce salad with mussel dressing."

On they swam around the island to Galleon Beach, where their grandparents lived.

"A council meeting," called up Miranda, "tonight in the Great Hall at the sea palace."

"It will be lovely to see the whole family, dear," answered Grandma. "We'll be there, with jellyfish mousse for dessert."

Miranda and Toby were rather tired by that time, so they floated home on their backs. When they reached the sea palace, they told the MerQueen and MerKing about the meeting. The MerKing, who liked eating more than meeting, sighed.

"At least mother makes wonderful jellyfish mousse."

The MerQueen sighed too. "We must clean the Great Hall." So she called together her cleaning staff: the crabs and clams and catfish. Soon the crabs were scuttling across the floor of the Great Hall, dusting and scraping off barnacles, jellyfish, and starfish. The clams crawled over the walls absorbing pebbles, sea moss and dust. And the catfish swam round and round, dusting the great council table with their long whiskers.

The MerKing went down to his vast cellar and brought out his best sea sacs wine. The MerQueen and Miranda gathered sea orchids and sea anemones for the table decoration, and Toby arranged the seating.

Finally, when the sun set over the mountains across the channel, the cousins arrived. The aunt and uncle and grandparents, who were too old to swim so far, came in a sea-green chariot drawn by twenty sea horses.

What a feast they had—it lasted several hours. There was singing and talking and catching up on news. Grandma's jellyfish mousse was very tasty; everyone had seconds.

After a while Miranda began to get restless. She looked at her father, raised her eyebrows and rolled her eyes. But the MerKing was enjoying eating too much to begin the meeting. And when Miranda whispered to her mother, the MerQueen said absently, "That's nice, dear," and turned back to her sister. "So then what did *he* say?"

After another hour Miranda, flushing an angry purple, swam up onto the table. "I've called this meeting because we have to do something about the sea monster trespassing in our caves. Since he came here a year ago, our lives have changed—his snores disturb our sleep and our meals. When he gets up and swims out to sea, we must hide in our palace and we can't sunbathe on our rocks or play in the waves. I'd like to see those shiny loops of his flat and still under the sea!" she finished with a flourish.

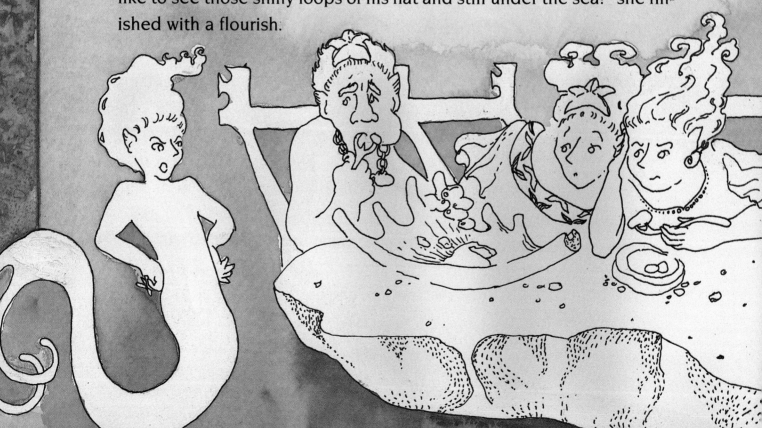

Her grandmother spoke: "Things are not the same as when I was a girl. How everything has changed with the coming of this monster and surely not for the better."

Her uncle spoke: "Perhaps this *is* a change for the better, my dear. We should not question change; we accept things as they are."

Miranda replied: "But why? I want to be free again, to do what I like, without fear."

Everyone began muttering and speaking out at once. Suddenly, her cousin Edward leaped up.

"I call the merpeople of Hornby Island to battle. I say we must protect our homeland. We must not allow invasions by foreigners who force us to change our ways or our customs." His voice rang out strong and true. "I will not rest till the monster's loops lie broken and bloody upon the sea! To war!"

"Hurray!" cried all the merpeople, making so much noise that Cuthbert stirred in his sleep, setting off ripples of waves through the palace and the Great Hall, upsetting flasks of wine and causing one young cousin to become violently seasick.

Preparations for Battle

Go to war they did. ("What about uniforms?" Robin reminded me.) First, they needed uniforms. Beatrice, the aunt who was a skilled seamstress, sewed up lovely uniforms of seaweed green with sunlit silver threads. All the cousins looked splendid.

Edward made them weapons—sharp spears, gleaming in the sun. Every morning at 6.00 a.m. the cousins in smart uniforms, flashing spears, swam up and down in battlelines for training.

One morning Toby said to Miranda, "I'm tired of getting up so early and swimming back and forth in lines every morning."

Miranda pulled herself up to her full height. "Then I will join the army." She had Beatrice make her a lovely uniform that showed off the colours and lines of her tail. She didn't really like getting up so early either, but she did it all the same.

After Edward inspected the uniforms and the presentation of arms, he set the battle day for the following Monday. The MerKing and MerQueen addressed the troops and off they all swam, first twenty cormorants, followed by thirty oyster catchers, and then thirty tall and stately herons. Next were the gleaming flanks of the mercousins escorted by ten electric eels, and twenty seals barking loudly, with twenty fierce-toothed sharks at the tail end.

They swam out to the open sea, and there they waited in splendid formation (except for Beatrice's son who held his spear in the wrong hand). Their spears glittered in the noon sun (they were a little late for the morning battle).

No Cuthbert.

"Next Tuesday," snapped Edward, "we meet again. Company dismissed!" And next Tuesday they all gathered again and swam out to the open sea. And, once again, no Cuthbert.

There is nothing more frustrating than a war and no one to fight.

The Battle-Finally

Finally Edward called his generals together—his two older brothers. They decided on a plan of attack. Edward sent ten electric eels down to Cuthbert. They gave him ten electric shocks. But all Cuthbert did was shiver and groan and turn over, causing tidal waves to wash over the battlelines, making everyone sputter and gasp.

Once again Edward called together his troops and sent the eels down to Cuthbert. This time there were twenty. . . . But all Cuthbert did was shudder and groan and roll over, sending an earthquake through the cave and upsetting the MerKing and MerQueen at tea.

Finally, the next Saturday, he sent down *thirty* electric eels. Cuthbert felt like thirty mosquitoes were stinging him.

("No," said Robin, "more like thirty bees!"

"You're right," I agreed, "thirty bees.")

Zing, zang, zong. Cuthbert woke. He was annoyed and grumpy, for he was in the middle of a nice nap. He shook out his loops and swam slowly out of his cave. He blinked in the bright sun at the flashing spears, then swam right into the open. Slowly he pulled his floppy loops up into seven shiny, black, perfect "O's", and stared around him in surprise.

"Forward!" cried Edward fiercely. Thirty spears gleamed in the sun—Beatrice's son still had his in the wrong hand. Two hit Cuthbert, drawing specks of blood from one of his lovely loops.

"Charge!" cried Edward, more fiercely. And twenty-eight spears were raised. But suddenly, two big tears splashed down from Cuthbert's large soft eyes. He opened his pink mouth and began to sob.

"Why are you attacking me? Why are you hurting me?" He licked the blood from his wounded loops. "Why are you so unfriendly? I'm

lonely. No one talks to me. I wanted to talk and play with you in the sea. But every time I opened my mouth you all disappeared. You hide all the time in the sea palace. No one will play with me, no one will talk to me. I've been so lonely. I...I...I miss my mummy. I want my mummy. Oh, why did I ever leave home?"

And Cuthbert sobbed and sobbed.

Soon the whole merarmy was sobbing, too. It was like being in a huge rain shower.

Then Miranda, who stood at the far end of the battle line, shouted-

("Where was Toby?" remembered Robin.

"He decided he didn't like war, and stayed home with the Mer-Queen in the sea palace," I explained.)

Miranda shouted, "Quiet!"

Everyone stopped sobbing, even Cuthbert, and looked at her. The sea calmed down.

"Mr. Sea Monster," Miranda addressed the sea monster whose lovely loops were drooping sadly.

"My name's Cuthbert," he interrupted shyly.

"Cuthbert, there's been a misunderstanding. When you opened your mouth to speak, we thought you wanted to eat us."

Cuthbert shook his head again. "Oh,no!"

"But then, you see,"continued Miranda firmly, "when you sleep way at the bottom of the caves, you snore and that shakes our sea palace and frightens us."

Cuthbert hung his head, then he brightened. "I've been sleeping on my back; maybe if I was tae sleep on my side I wouldn't snore."

The troops cheered. "Hurray for Cuthbert!"

Edward leaped up. "War is over; I declare Peace. Hurray for Cuthbert!"

Cuthbert perked up, his loops stiffened and shone in the sun. He smiled. "Could we be friends? Perhaps I could help you. I could bring you thirty fish a week, if you like, for your Sunday dinner."

The MerKing, who had been standing on the big cliff watching the battle, said, "Let's start tomorrow."

The MerQueen, who had come back with Toby, said politely, "Perhaps you would join us for Sunday dinner, Cuthbert."

"Oh," said Cuthbert, crestfallen, "thirty fish are no enough, I can eat at least a hundred and sixty." He thought for a minute. "I could bring my fish and eat with you."

"That would be lovely," said the MerQueen.

(And Robin said, "They could have a huge fish cake or even fish pie, as big as this . . ."

"Good idea," I said quickly.)

Instead of a battle, they had a big party. Cuthbert was the life of the party. First, the cousins swam in and out of his loops, playing tag, then Miranda and Toby rode them up and down like a roller coaster.

What a day! what a party!

("Wish I could ride on that roller coaster," said Robin wistfully.)

A few days later Cuthbert wrote his first letter home:

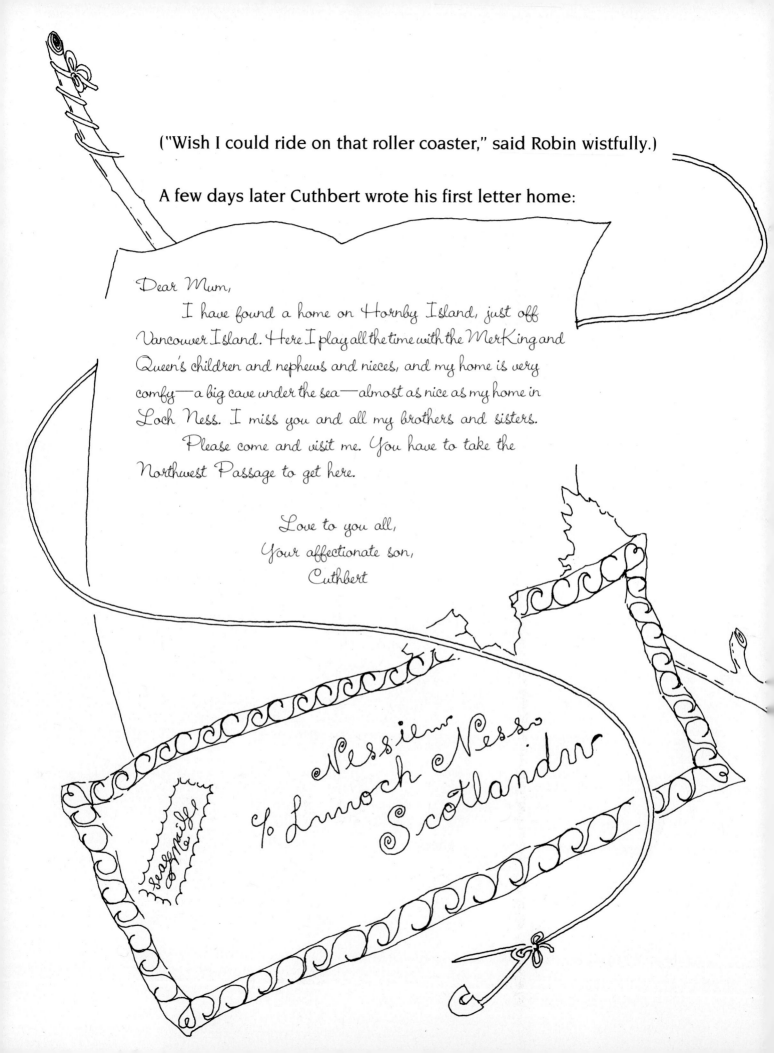

Dear Mum,

I have found a home on Hornby Island, just off Vancouver Island. Here I play all the time with the Mer King and Queen's children and nephews and nieces, and my home is very comfy—a big cave under the sea—almost as nice as my home in Loch Ness. I miss you and all my brothers and sisters.

Please come and visit me. You have to take the Northwest Passage to get here.

Love to you all,
Your affectionate son,
Cuthbert

Nessie
℅ Lurnock Ness
Scotland